This Book Belongs To

. . . .

T J

and the Great Snail Show

Rose Impey
Anna Currey

Hodder
Children's
Books

a division of Hodder Headline plc

For Ruth and Sandra

Chapter One

Josie wouldn't go to sleep because Pinkie had been left out in the rain. Mum sent TJ to find him. "Be quick," she said.

TJ ran down the path.
There were snails all over the
place.
She shone the torch in front of her,
taking care not to step on any.

TJ found Pinkie on the climbing frame. He was wet through.

TJ carried him in by his ears,
dripping on the carpet.

"Don't bring him over here,"
Mum told TJ. "He's far too wet."

Josie started to cry.
"Want Pinkie," she said.

TJ sat him on her radiator
to dry out.
"He'll be as good as new
tomorrow," Mum told her.

When TJ woke up, the first thing she saw was Pinkie with a snail sitting on his head.

The snail had a beautiful shell; brown and yellow striped, like a humbug.

TJ carried the snail downstairs.
Mum said, "Put it back in the
garden."
Mum didn't like creepy-crawlies.

But TJ said, "She's not an *it*, she's
a *her*. I want to keep her."

TJ loved the snail.
She called her Humbug and sat
her in an empty cereal packet
while she had breakfast.

Then TJ went outside to find
some breakfast for Humbug.
Snails don't eat cereals.

Chapter Two

When TJ's friends, Gemma and Jake, came to play, they wanted a snail too. They all went out into the garden on a snail hunt.

Mrs Bee told them where to look.
"Dark and damp places, that's
what snails like," she said.

They looked under flowerpots,
against walls, and behind the
dustbin.

They found lots of snails but
none of them were as beautiful
as Humbug.

Some of the shells were empty.
The birds had eaten the snails.
"Poor snails," said Gemma.

"Poor birds," said Jake. He didn't
fancy snails for breakfast.

Gemma found a really small
snail. She called it Teeny-Weeny.

But Jake chose the biggest he
could find.

"It's huge," said TJ. "What are
you going to call it?"
"Sumo," said Jake. Because it
reminded him of the big fat sumo
wrestlers he'd seen on TV.

TJ and Gemma went to get some boxes from Mum, to make homes for Humbug and Teeny-Weeny.

They filled them with grass and moss and stones, then put a roof on each, so it would be dark inside.

Jake didn't bother to make a house for his snail.
He spent all his time looking for food to fatten up Sumo.

He ran home to ask his mum for some lettuce leaves.

If Jake was quiet and put his ear
very close, he could hear Sumo
tearing it into pieces.
"Come and listen," he called to
the others.

"Don't you think he's big enough already?" said Gemma.

"No way," said Jake. "He's going to be the most gigantic, colossal, enormous, huge, mega-massive snail in the world."

"Lovely," said TJ, screwing up her nose.

Chapter Three

The next day, after school, when Gemma and Jake came round to play, they brought their snails with them.

TJ and Gemma made gardens
for Humbug and Teeny-Weeny,
with a path and a front gate. TJ
even put a pretend pond
in hers.

Jake was busy making a wrestling ring. He put lots of other snails in the ring with Sumo.

But the snails just climbed out. They didn't seem interested in wrestling.

Neither did Sumo.
He was only interested in eating
. . . and sleeping.

Jake kept trying to wake him
up with a twig.

"Don't do that," said Gemma.
"How would you like it if a great
big giant poked you with a stick?"
Jake *wouldn't* have liked it,
so he didn't do it anymore.

The next day Abi came round
to play. When she saw everyone's
pet snails, she wanted one too.

She searched all afternoon.
Abi wanted hers to be the very
best.

But she couldn't
find one as big
as Sumo . . .

or one as
beautiful as
Humbug . . .

or one as small
and sweet as
Teeny-Weeny.

But Abi did find
a snail that
moved faster
than the others.

Every time she put
him in one place
he turned round
and headed off
somewhere else.

"Watch him
go," Abi told
Jake. "He's
so fast."

"You call that fast?" said Jake.
"Well, he's fast for a snail,"
said Abi.

"I'm going to call him Speedy,
the fastest snail in town.

Chapter Four

"When TJ's friend Danny heard about the snail club, he wanted to join too.

"It's not exactly a club," said TJ.
"Anyway, you'll have to find a
snail first."
Mrs Bee looked over the fence.
"Has everyone gone snail mad
round here?" she said.

Abi wanted them to have snail
races, but Mrs Bee hadn't
forgotten the sunflower race.
TJ and Abi had almost fallen out
over that.

"Why don't you have a Snail
Show instead?" she suggested.
"And I'll give everyone a prize."

"Yeah!" they all squealed.

At the weekend everyone brought
their snails to TJ's house.
Mrs Bee came round, and Jan
from next door with the baby.

And TJ's friend Laura and her
mum came, too.
They all went round and looked
at the snails and clapped when
Mrs Bee gave them their prizes.

TJ's snail, Humbug, was The
Most Beautiful Snail in the show.

Gemma's snail, Teeny-Weeny,
was The Smallest Snail.

Jake's snail, Sumo, was
The Biggest Snail by far.

He was big enough to give
some of the smaller snails
rides on his back.

Danny's snail, Gladiator, was The Best Climber in the show. It could even climb up a knitting needle and balance on the top.

Abi made a little racing track. Her snail always won because the other snails kept wandering off the track or going to sleep.

Speedy, was definitely The Fastest Snail in the show.

Chapter Five

So everyone was happy, because everyone had won.

Mum said they could all stay for tea. She made a proper Snail Tea Party, with curly-wurly sandwiches and meringues. But the snails weren't invited.

When TJ and her friends went out into the garden to collect their snails, they'd all disappeared.

"They've probably gone back to their real homes," said Mrs Bee.

"Don't worry there'll be plenty more snails to find tomorrow."

Jake wasn't worried. He was getting bored with snails.
"They don't do much, do they?" he said.
"No," agreed Mrs Bee. "They're just eating machines, really."

But TJ was sorry to lose
Humbug. Tomorrow she'd look
for her. She'd left a silver trail
for TJ to follow, all down the
garden path.